THE SAWFIN STICKLEBACK
A Very Fishy Story

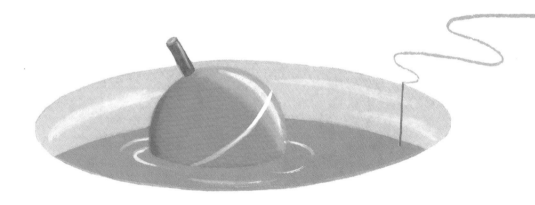

Catherine Friend ◆ *Illustrated by* Dan Yaccarino

Hyperion Books for Children
New York

For information address Hyperion Books for Children,
114 Fifth Avenue, New York, New York 10011.

FIRST EDITION
1 3 5 7 9 10 8 6 4 2

Library of Congress Cataloging-in-Publication Data

Friend, Catherine.
The Sawfin Stickleback: a very fishy story / Catherine Friend;
illustrated by Dan Yaccarino – 1st ed.
p. cm.
Summary: People still talk about the time Katie and her little brother, Mark, almost caught
the gigantic Sawfin Stickleback while ice fishing with their grandfather.
ISBN 1-56282-473-2 (trade) – ISBN 1-56282-474-0 (lib. bdg.)
[1. Ice fishing – Fiction. 2. Fishing – fiction. 3. Brothers and sisters – Fiction.
4. Grandfathers – Fiction.] I. Yaccarino, Dan, ill. II. Title.
PZ7.F91523Saw 1994 [E] – dc20 93-47151 CIP AC

For Melissa
—C. F.

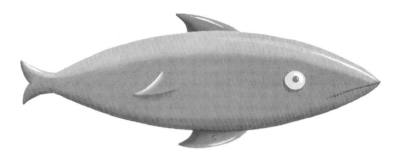

For my grandparents
—D. Y.

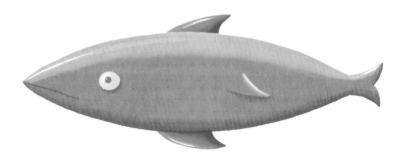

P eople still talk about the time my little brother Mark caught the gigantic Sawfin Stickleback, the most feared fish in Amber Lake.

It happened the first time Mark came ice fishing with Grandpa and me. We sat snug and warm in Grandpa's icehouse on top of frozen Amber Lake. Wood crackled in the stove, and shifting ice groaned underneath us. We were over Grandpa's favorite fishing spot, but nothing was happening. We stared at our bobbers.

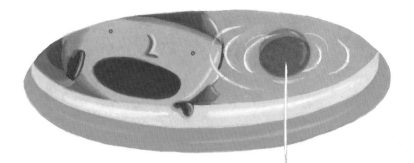

"Hey!" I hollered down my ice hole.
"Anybody down there?" The ice, two feet
thick, shimmered a strange blue and white.
The water was dark and mysterious.
What could be lurking below? Maybe fish
so big they could swallow us whole!

Mark stuck his head down his ice hole.

"Katie! I see something," he said,
jumping back.

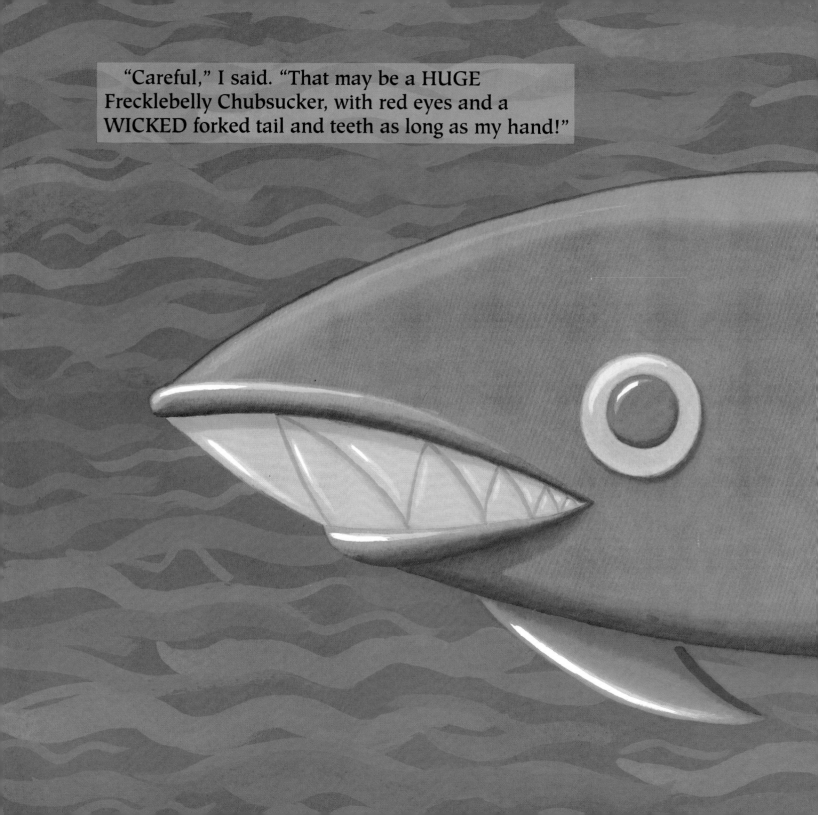

"Careful," I said. "That may be a HUGE Frecklebelly Chubsucker, with red eyes and a WICKED forked tail and teeth as long as my hand!"

Mark's mouth fell open. Was there really such a fish?

Grandpa winked at me and asked Mark what he would do if he caught a Frecklebelly Chubsucker.

"I'd have all of us grab on to the line and pull and pull and pull," he said.

Mark snuggled back down into Grandpa's old green stuffed chair to watch his bobber. The warm smell of burning wood filled the icehouse. The cold wind whistled outside. We watched for what seemed like hours, but nothing happened. Mark looked down his ice hole again.

"There it is!" he cried.

"Watch out," I said. "That may be a
GIGANTIC Ninespine Cisco with
pink eyes and HORRIBLE blue spiky
scales and teeth as long as my arm!
He's so big he wouldn't even fit through
the hole in the ice!"

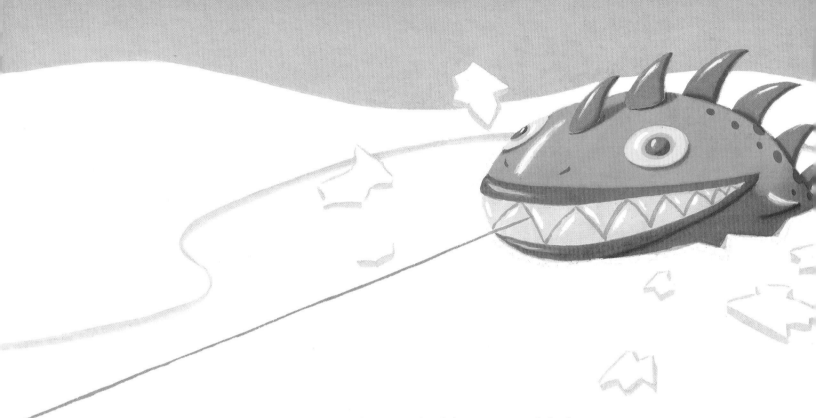

Mark's eyes got as big as bobbers. Could there really be such a fish?

Grandpa winked at me and asked Mark what he would do if he caught a Ninespine Cisco.

Mark looked down at the icehouse floor. "I'd cut a bigger hole in the floor, then a bigger hole in the ice," he said. "I'd hook my fishing line to your pickup and we'd yank that fish right out of the water!"

Grandpa caught two fish. Mark and I still hadn't caught anything. Mark looked down the eerie blue hole again.

"Katie, it's back!" he cried.

"Careful," I said. "That may be a TOTALLY HUMONGOUS Sawfin Stickleback with BULGING eyes and horrible spines down his back and teeth as long as my leg! He's so big that one eye would fill up the ice hole!"

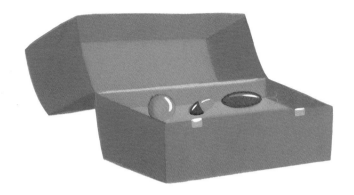

Grandpa winked and asked Mark what he would do if he caught a Sawfin Stickleback.

"I'd find my new red scissors in my tackle box and cut the line."

Grandpa laughed. "Well, you may have to do that. Your bobber just disappeared."

Mark and I shrieked and ran for his fishing pole. "Help!" Mark yelled. "What do I do?"

"Grab your line and jerk it hard to set the hook!" Grandpa said.

Mark jerked the line and tried to hold it tight, but it just slipped through his hands.

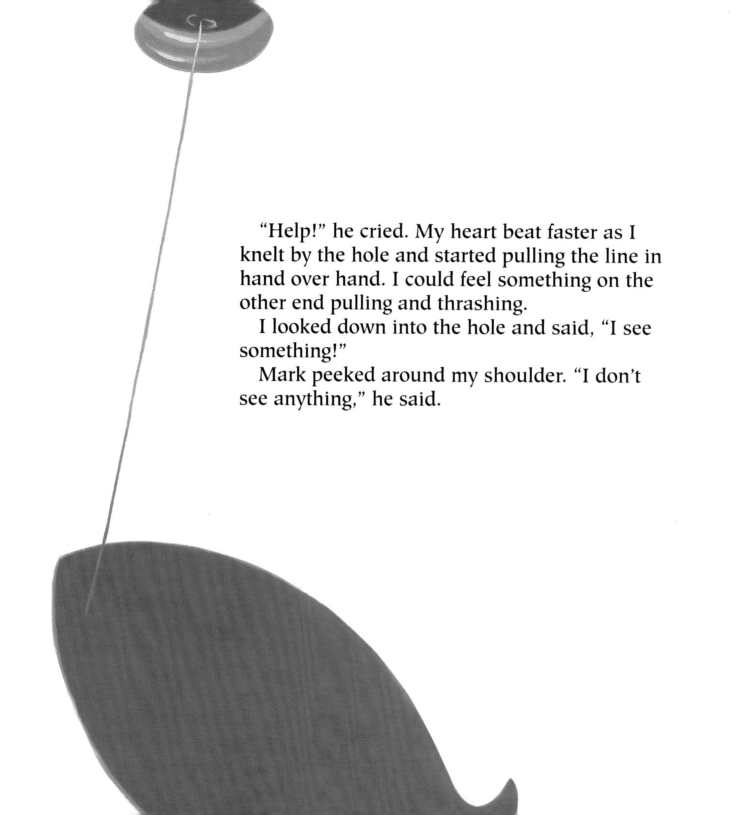

"Help!" he cried. My heart beat faster as I knelt by the hole and started pulling the line in hand over hand. I could feel something on the other end pulling and thrashing.

I looked down into the hole and said, "I see something!"

Mark peeked around my shoulder. "I don't see anything," he said.

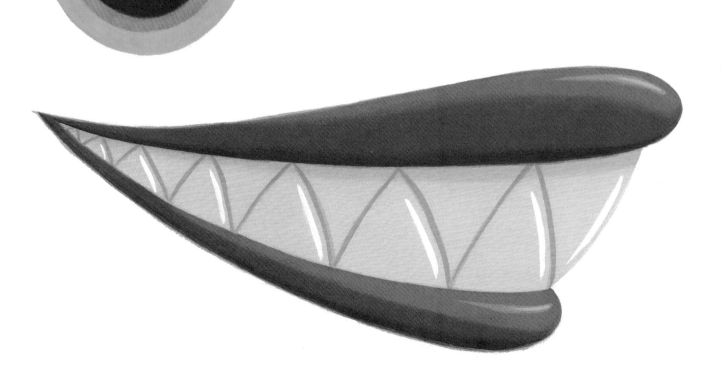

I kept pulling in the line, my hands wet from the freezing water.

"Wait! What's that?" Mark shouted.

"An eye!" I said. "There's a GIGANTIC eye staring at us!"

Mark took a step back. In fact, he took two steps back.

My arms were shaking and my teeth were chattering, but I was determined. The fish thrashed from side to side and shot up and down. It was a real tug-of-war.

"Teeth!" I cried. "I see teeth, HUGE teeth!"

That was enough for Mark. He turned his back
and flew to his tackle box. "My scissors! Where
are my scissors?"

Just then Mark's fish popped up through the
hole. Grandpa winked at me. "Whoa!" he said.
"Look out for those teeth!"

"I'll save us, Katie!" Mark cried. "I've got to find my scissors!"

"It's trying to come up through the hole!" I said.

"They're in here somewhere!" Mark cried. "Hang on!"

Grandpa quickly took the fish off the hook and slipped it and the line back into the water. I stuffed the bobber into my pocket.

"Found 'em!" Mark cried. He ran to the hole, snipped the line, then sank to his knees. We watched the line sink out of sight. "Boy, that was close," he said.

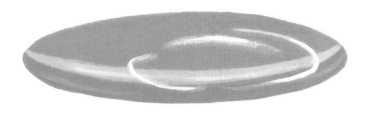

"You saved us, Mark!" I said.

Grandpa shook his head. "That sure was a whopper."

Mark was so excited, all he could do was run around in circles. "I hooked a whopper! A Sawfin Stickleback for sure!"

That's how the story of Mark's Sawfin Stickleback got started. And every time Mark tells the story, that fish gets bigger

and BIGGER

and BIGGER!

Now that's what I call a *real* fish story.